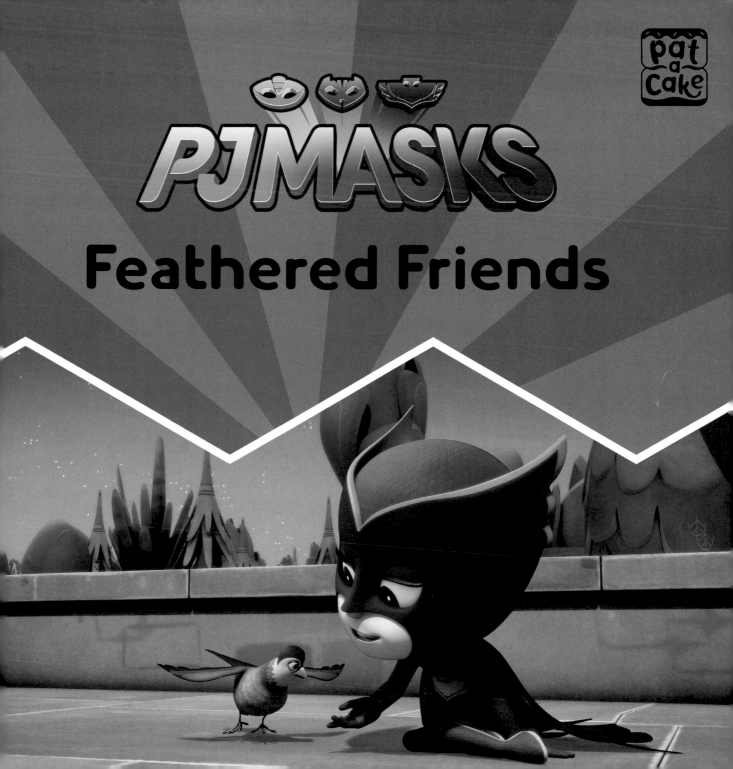

PJMASKS

Feathered Friends

Amaya and Connor were playing at Greg's house.

"Come on, Lionel," said Greg. "That's a good lizard."

His little green pet blinked up at him, then reached out to nibble some food.

"I wish I had a pet," sighed Amaya. "They're lots of fun."

"They're hard work, too," Greg reminded her.

The friends' wrist bracelets started to flash.

Weeoo-weeoo-weeoo!

"It's the alarm signal," gasped Connor. "Someone is trying to break into our HQ!"

"We've got to go!" said Amaya.

PJ MASKS ARE ON THEIR WAY, INTO THE NIGHT TO SAVE THE DAY!

NIGHT IN THE CITY. A BRAVE BAND OF HEROES IS READY TO FACE FIENDISH VILLAINS TO STOP THEM MESSING WITH YOUR DAY.

AMAYA BECOMES . . . *OWLETTE!*

CONNOR BECOMES .

ATBOY!

GREG BECOMES . . . GEKKO!

The PJ Masks rushed into the HQ.
Whoosh! Something was already inside! It had wings and a feathery tail.
"That's no intruder," cried Catboy, "look, it's a bird!"
The bird fluttered down from the roof, then began to coo softly in Owlette's ear.

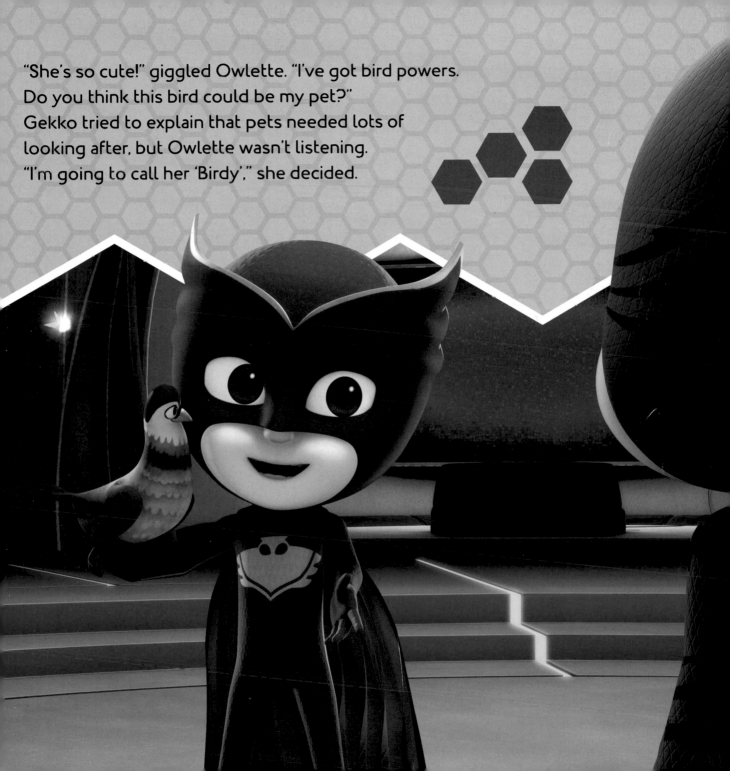

"She's so cute!" giggled Owlette. "I've got bird powers.
Do you think this bird could be my pet?"
Gekko tried to explain that pets needed lots of
looking after, but Owlette wasn't listening.
"I'm going to call her 'Birdy'," she decided.

But somebody else had their eyes on Owlette's new pet. Luna Girl!

"You think that looking after a pet is easy?" Luna Girl muttered. "I know different!" She pressed a button on her Luna-Magnet. It was time to put her sneaky plan into action . . .

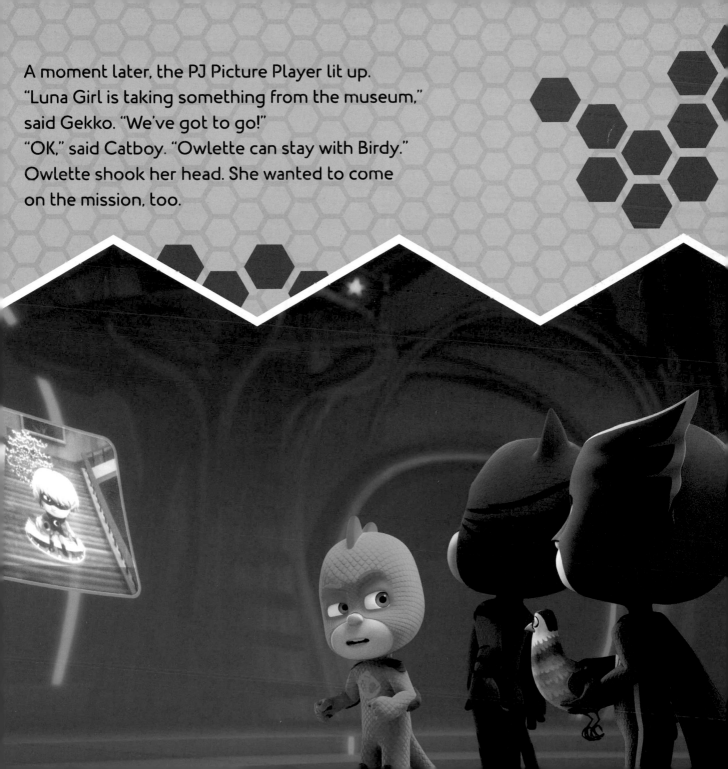

A moment later, the PJ Picture Player lit up.
"Luna Girl is taking something from the museum,"
said Gekko. "We've got to go!"
"OK," said Catboy. "Owlette can stay with Birdy."
Owlette shook her head. She wanted to come
on the mission, too.

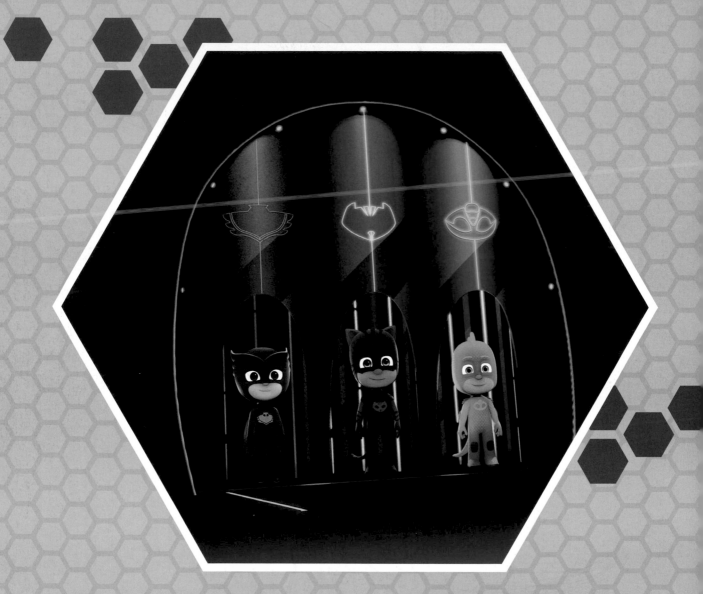

The PJ Masks rushed to the Owl Glider. It didn't take long to find Luna Girl.
"What have you taken from the museum?" shouted Owlette.
Luna Girl held up a vase. "Just something for my Luna Lair."

While the heroes were chasing after the stolen vase, Birdy was hard at work. Luna Girl had made Birdy go to the PJ Masks' HQ in order to hide Luna-Crystals. If Birdy could hide enough crystals in the HQ, the villain would be able to use them to turn it into a massive Luna-Magnet!

"Phase one complete," said Luna Girl, letting the vase fall. Catboy caught it just in time.

When the PJ Masks got back to their HQ, Birdy had made a terrible mess. "Why did she do this?" gasped Owlette. "Maybe it's because you left her alone?" said Gekko. "Pets need lots of attention." Owlette sighed. Pets were meant to be fun. Tidying up mess was no fun at all!

The alarm flashed again. Now Luna Girl had broken into the zoo!
"Let's go," urged Catboy.
"What about Birdy?" asked Gekko.
Owlette reached out for her feathered friend.
"She can come, too!"

As soon as the heroes arrived, Luna Girl disappeared into the shadows.
"Hmm," frowned Catboy. "She isn't usually that easy to scare off."
Owlette led the way into the zoo. Birdy was left behind in the Owl Glider.

Luna Girl tiptoed up to the PJ pet.
"Has Owlette left you all alone?" she whispered, tucking
more Luna Crystals under Birdy's wing.

When the PJ Masks came back to the HQ after checking the zoo, Owlette
couldn't understand why Birdy looked so sad.
"Birdy needs some attention," said Gekko. "And maybe you should feed her?"

Owlette fetched a bowl of food for Birdy. She was just about
to take a peck when . . . another call came in for the PJ Masks!

Owlette took the bowl away. The heroes needed to **go, go, go!**
"What about Birdy's food?" asked Gekko. "She seems hungry."
"We need to deal with Luna Girl," said Owlette, jumping into the Cat-Car.

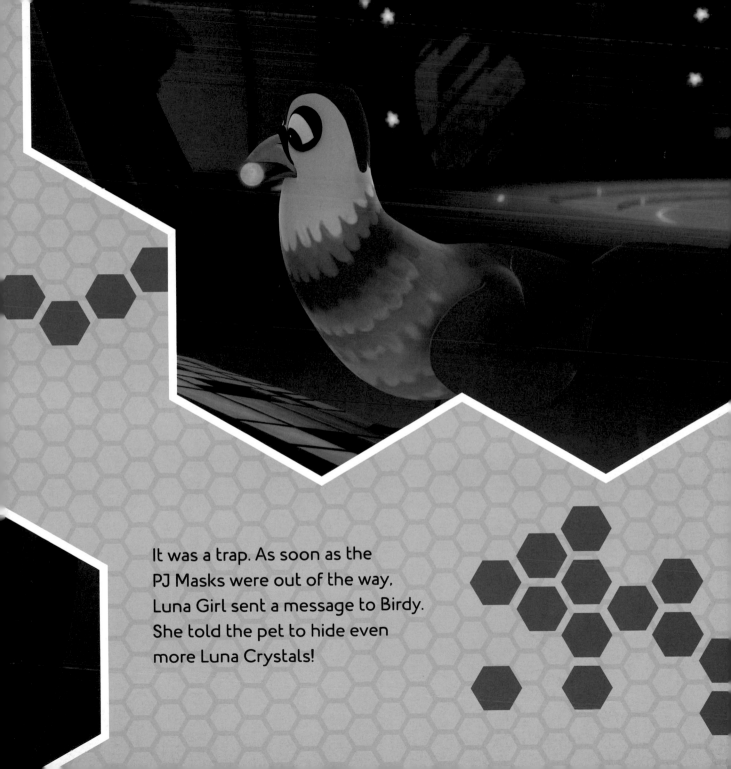

It was a trap. As soon as the
PJ Masks were out of the way,
Luna Girl sent a message to Birdy.
She told the pet to hide even
more Luna Crystals!

Luna Girl pressed a button to activate the Luna Crystals. The Cat-Car screeched to a halt. "What's wrong with our HQ?" shouted Catboy. "I've turned it into a giant Luna-Magnet," laughed Luna Girl, "thanks to that bird!"

"Birdy did this?" cried Owlette. "I don't believe it!"
"You're such a bad pet owner," nodded Luna Girl.
"Birdy put my Luna Crystals inside your HQ. Ha!"
Owlette hung her head. If only she had looked after her pet better!
"If you can hear me, I'm sorry," she called. "I won't let you down again."

Catboy pointed to the sky. Birdy was flying towards Owlette.
She had escaped and wanted to be friends.

Luna Girl's giant magnet was starting to work. Cars, buses and street signs all got dragged towards the park gates.

BANG! CLUNK! CRASH!

"The gates won't hold for long," warned Owlette.
"We have to stop this!" shouted Catboy.

"Super Gekko Muscles!"

Gekko used his super strength to keep the gates shut. Catboy joined in.

"I need to find a way into the HQ," said Owlette. Birdy spread her wings. She wanted to help, too!

Birdy was a pet with a plan. She whistled in Owlette's ear.

"OK," nodded the hero. "I believe in you!"

Birdy flew down towards Luna Girl, then gave her a peck on the bottom.

"Ow!"

The baddie tried to chase after the pet, but she got sucked into the HQ's red beam. Now she was trapped!

Quick as a flash, Birdy darted inside the HQ and collected all of the Luna Crystals.
The Luna-Magnet stopped working.
"What happened to my Luna Power?" bellowed Luna Girl.
"My pet Birdy happened!' replied Owlette.
Gekko and Catboy cheered.

After that, Amaya played with Birdy every day. She even taught her tricks.
"Teaching a pet takes a lot of work," said Greg.
Birdy found a place to perch, then nodded her head.
Amaya giggled at Greg. "Good trick, Birdy!"

PJ MASKS ALL SHOUT HOORAY.
'CAUSE IN THE NIGHT, WE SAVED THE DAY!

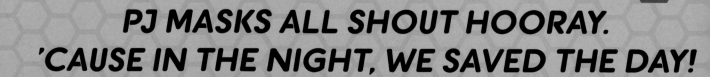